For Mat, and helpful cups of tea in the early hours
— O. H.

For Linda, my creative guardian angel. Her generosity has
helped me sleep a little better at night. Thank you
— C. P.

tiger tales
5 River Road, Suite 128, Wilton, CT 06897
Published in the United States 2017
Originally published in Great Britain 2017
by Little Tiger Press
Text by Owen Hart
Text copyright © 2017 Little Tiger Press
Illustrations copyright © 2017 Caroline Pedler
ISBN-13: 978-1-68010-066-2
ISBN-10: 1-68010-066-1
Printed in China
LTP/1400/1809/0217

For more insight and activities, visit us at www.tigertalesbooks.com

I Can't Sleep!

by Owen Hart • Illustrated by Caroline Pedler

tiger tales

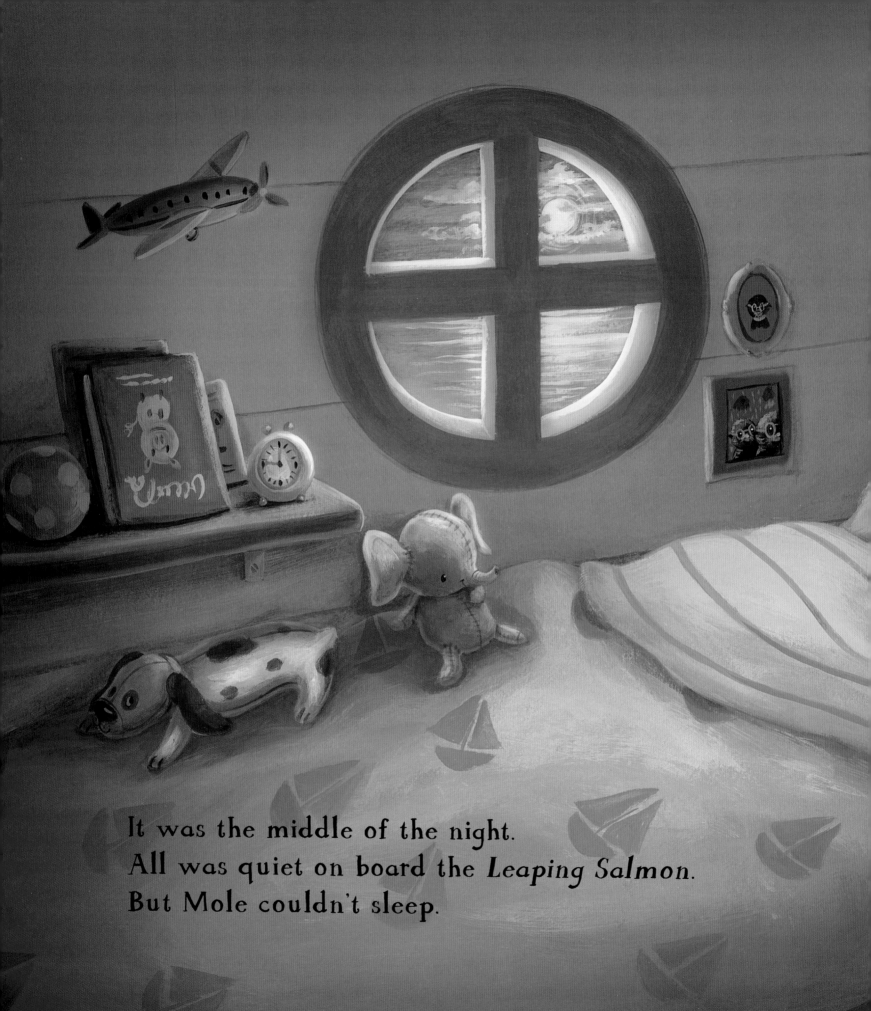

It was the middle of the night.
All was quiet on board the *Leaping Salmon.*
But Mole couldn't sleep.

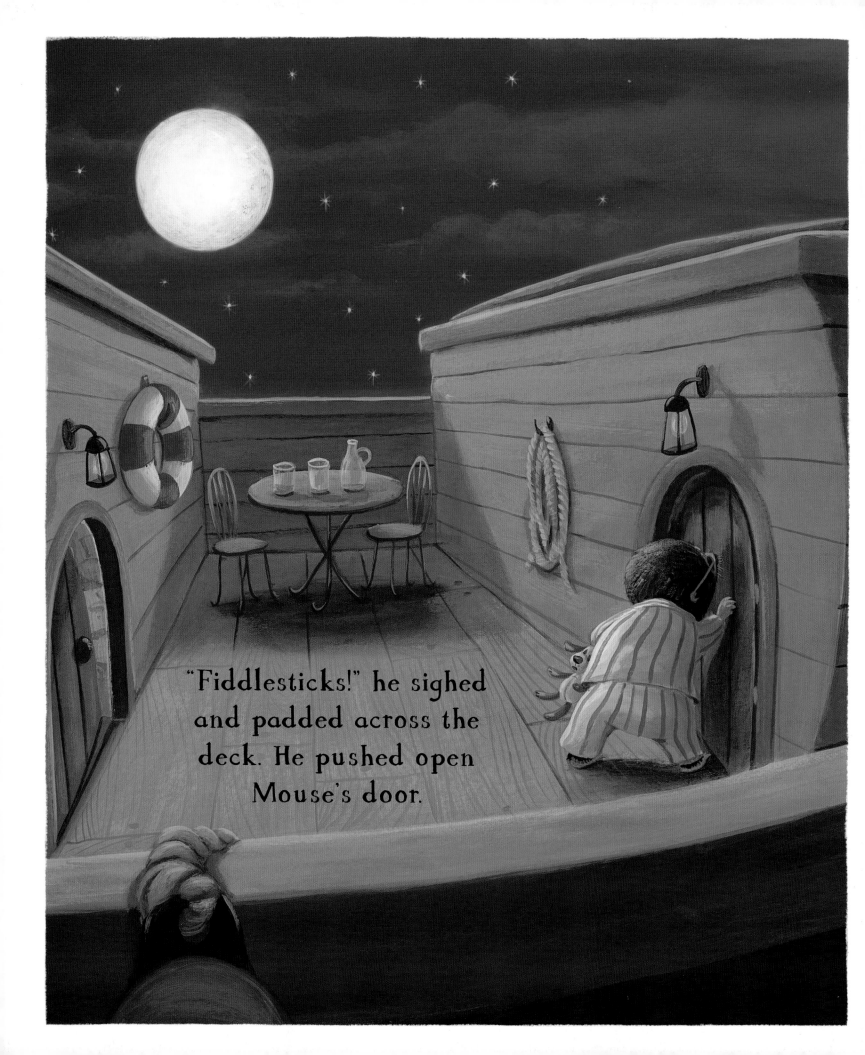

"Fiddlesticks!" he sighed and padded across the deck. He pushed open Mouse's door.

"Mouse! Mouse!" he called. "I can't sleep.
Can I come in here with you?"
    Mouse yawned and peered at Mole in the moonlight.
"Sure," he said. "Don't forget your blanket."

While Mole plumped
up the pillows,
Mouse had an idea.
"Let's read a bedtime story,"
he said.
"Yippee!" cheered Mole.

As Mouse turned the pages,
Mole began to feel sleepy.
But as soon as they reached
the happily ever after,
Mole cried, "It's too short!
Can we read another one?"

Mole picked a second book, and Mouse began to read.
But then Mole gave a sudden squeak.
"Too scary!" he cried.
"This won't help me sleep!"

So Mouse read a third story,
about a boat just like theirs.
"Ahhh," sighed Mole. "That was just right."
And he settled down to sleep.

But Mole wasn't
quiet for long.
"Mouse! Mouse!"
he called.
"I still can't sleep!"

"Why not?" asked Mouse.
"It's too dark!" said Mole.
"And I can't stop thinking about the scary story."

Mouse turned on the
lamp. A soft glow
filled the room,
and soon Mole was
silent again . . .

. . . but only for awhile.
"Mouse!" he cried. "Now it's too bright!"

Luckily, Mouse had a better idea.
He opened the door to the cubby above
his bed and took out a large piece of paper.
"That won't help me sleep!" said Mole.
"Watch," said Mouse.

Mouse began to
cut the paper.
Mole looked on
in wonder.

With a tuck
and a fold,
Mouse had
made the
perfect
lampshade.

"Wow—look at that!" exclaimed Mole as stars and moons danced on the walls. "It's just right." And he rolled over with a happy sigh.

But Mole didn't stay still for long.
"Mouse! Mouse!" he called.
"I STILL can't sleep. I'm too cold!"

Mouse looked in the drawer under his bed and took out a warm blanket. "You can use this," he said. Mole pulled the blanket right up to his chin and closed his tired eyes.

"Mouse!" he squeaked. "Now I'm too hot!" "Even without the blanket?" asked Mouse. "Yes!" fretted Mole.

So Mouse had his best idea of all. "But I'll need your help," he told Mole. Together, they moved the chair . . .

and dragged the dresser . . .

and tugged at the trunk.

With one last push, the bed was
right next to the open window.
"That's perfect," said Mole.
"Thank you, Mouse."
And he snuggled under the covers.

At last all was peaceful.
The river lapped gently.
A frog croaked softly.
And everything was quiet
aboard the *Leaping Salmon*.

But not for long . . . .

"Mole! Mole!"
called Mouse.
"I can't sleep!"

It wasn't too dark
or too light.

And it wasn't too
hot or too cold.

What could be wrong?

"Mole!" cried Mouse.
"STOP THAT SNORING!"